Wisdom Publications
199 Elm Street
Somerville, MA 02144 USA
wisdomexperience.org

Library of Congress Cataloging-in-Publication Data is available.
LCCN 2022935759

ISBN 978-1-61429-792-5   ebook ISBN 978-1-61429-816-8

26 25 24 23 22   5 4 3 2 1

Cover and interior design by Katrina Damkoehler. Photo editing by Gretchen LeMaistre.

Printed on acid-free paper that meets the guidelines for permanence and durability of the
Production Guidelines for Book Longevity of the Council on Library Resources.

Printed in Malaysia.

Adventures in Kindness

LUMI

MOLLY COXE

Wisdom

One day, Lumi asked a tiny moon, "Why am I here?"

"You are here to help others," said the moon, beaming.

"But I'm so small," said Lumi.

"True, but you are connected to all radiant beings, large and small. Can you feel it?"

Lumi closed her eyes. She felt it.

"Emaho!" the moon exclaimed.

"Ema . . . ?"

"Emaho! Isn't it wonderful!"

"It is! Emaho!" Lumi exclaimed.

Lumi set out to find someone who needed help. It didn't take long.

On a lush planet nearby, a family of flower fairies was gathering pollen to make medicine. "It's too windy. The pollen is blowing away," they shouted.

With wisps of shimmering light, Lumi gathered the pollen.

The fairies swept the pollen off of Lumi into big baskets. Then they mixed it with dried flowers and two drops of honey to make the medicine. They shared it with everyone who needed it. Emaho!

Lumi set out to find someone else who needed help. It didn't take long.

On a frozen planet, two bands of warriors were shouting hurtful words at each other, preparing for battle.

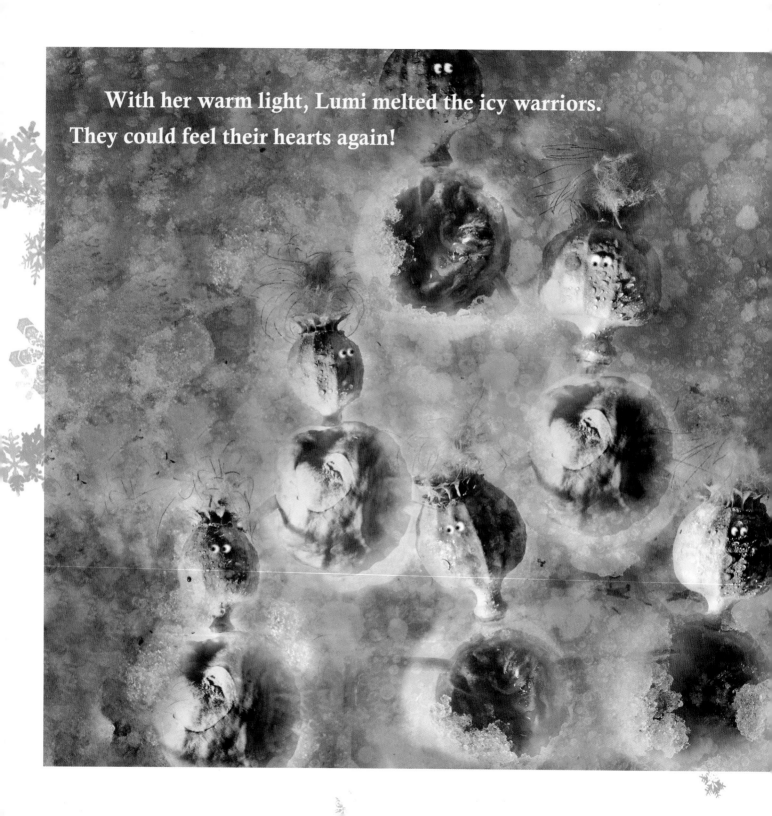

With her warm light, Lumi melted the icy warriors.
They could feel their hearts again!

Enemies became friends. Some even fell in love! Emaho!

Lumi set out to find someone else who needed help. It didn't take long.

A greedy monster was sucking up the stars illuminating a peaceful planet. "Excuse me, Mr. Monster, could you please stop stealing our stars?" the leader of the peaceful beings inquired politely.

The monster didn't stop.

The peaceful beings started to cry: they didn't want to live in the dark, on a planet without stars.

Luckily, Lumi had a bright idea: "I bet you can't steal me!" she teased the monster.

The monster stopped stealing stars and started chasing Lumi. It tried to suck her up, but it couldn't. Lumi was too quick.

Lumi led the monster to a galaxy where it could suck up stars for a billion years without bothering anyone. It's probably still there today. Emaho!

Lumi set out to find someone else who needed help. It didn't take long.

A colony of sea squirts was bobbing on the surface of a watery planet. "Why are you up here?" Lumi asked. "Don't you live underwater?"

"Yes!" said one of the squirts. "Our home is on a reef. We are very attached to it, and it isn't fair!"

"What isn't fair?" asked Lumi.

"The smoke! It's blocking the light we need to glow and grow. We have to look for a new home!"

"No, you don't!" said Lumi. "Follow me!"

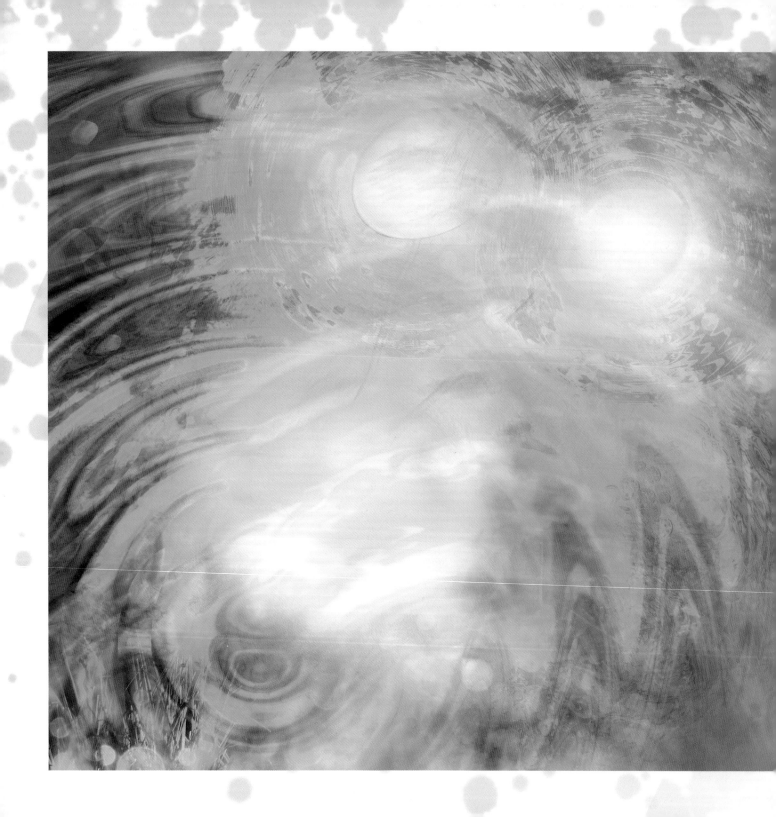

Diving deep below the surface of the sea, Lumi radiated wave after wave of rainbow light.

Soon, all the sea squirts were back home on the reef, glowing and growing again! They even created new kinds of squirts. Emaho!

Lumi set out to find someone else who needed help. It didn't take long. A storm was roiling the universe, upsetting everything.

This time, Lumi didn't know how to help. She was too small. It was too much.

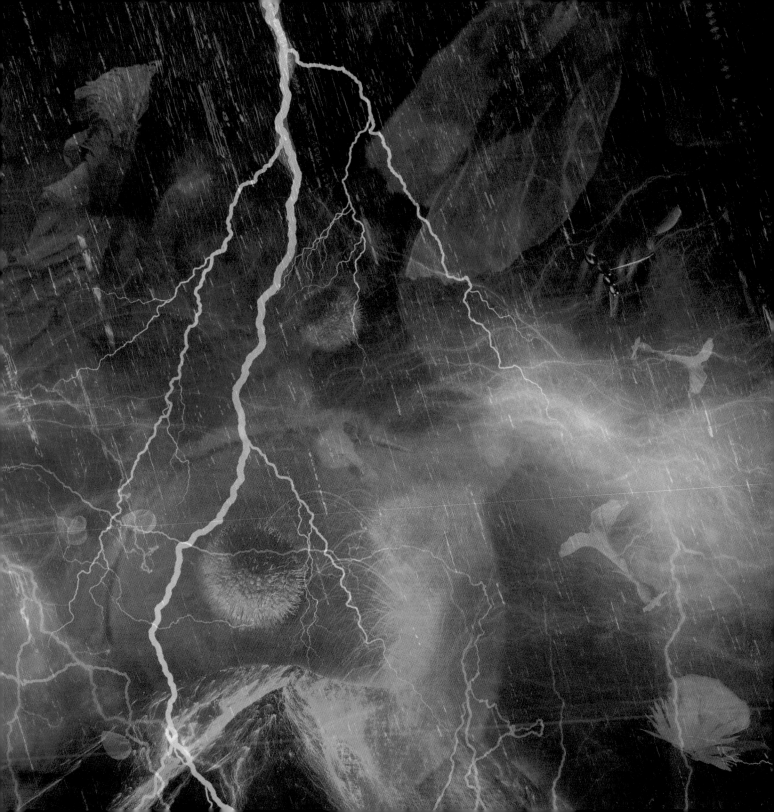

Lumi hid. She thought she might hide forever.

Then she remembered what the moon told her: "You are connected to all radiant beings, large and small."

Lumi imagined herself surrounded by an infinite number of benevolent beings.

Together, they transformed the storm into sparkling stardust—
stardust that would create new worlds!

Lumi felt grateful to be part of a universe where such amazing and wonderful things could happen. She found the tiny moon. They celebrated the end of the storm and sang songs with their friends until bedtime. Emaho!

Lumi's Song

As I wander, near and far,
Can you see me? I'm a star.
I can see you, shining bright.
Together, we light up the night.
Is it my imagination?
Are we all one constellation?
Emaho!

To hear Lumi's song
and learn more about her world,
*visit **lumiverse.org.***